Ellen Mackay Hutchinson

Songs and Lyrics

Ellen Mackay Hutchinson

Songs and Lyrics

ISBN/EAN: 9783744773485

Printed in Europe, USA, Canada, Australia, Japan

Cover: Foto ©Andreas Hilbeck / pixelio.de

More available books at **www.hansebooks.com**

HER PICTURE.

SONGS AND LYRICS

BY

ELLEN MACKAY HUTCHINSON

WITH FRONTISPIECE FROM A PAINTING
BY GEORGE H. BOUGHTON

BOSTON

JAMES R. OSGOOD AND COMPANY

1881

Univeristy Press:
John Wilson and Son, Cambridge.

TO

ELLEN SHEFFIELD PHELPS

CONTENTS.

INDEX OF FIRST LINES.

MOTH-SONG.

WHAT dost thou here,
Thou dusky courtier,
Within the pinky palace of the rose ?
Here is no bed for thee,
No honeyed spicery, —
But for the golden bee,
And the gay wind, and me
Its sweetness grows.
Rover, thou dost forget; —
Seek thou the passion-flower
Bloom of one twilight hour.
Haste, thou art late !
Its hidden savors wait.

For thee is spread
Its soft, purple coverlet ;
  Moth, art thou sped ?
— Dim as a ghost he flies
Through the night mysteries.

II.

HER PICTURE.

AUTUMN was cold in Plymouth town:
  The wind ran round the shore,
Now softly passing up and down,
    Now wild and fierce and fleet,
      Wavering overhead,
    Moaning in the narrow street
      As one beside the dead.

The leaves of wrinkled gold and brown
  Fluttered here and there,
  But not quite heedless where;
For as in hood and sad-hued gown
  The Rose of Plymouth took the air,
They whirled, and whirled, and fell to rest

Upon her gentle breast,
Then on the happy earth her foot had pressed.

Autumn is wild in Plymouth town,
Barren and bleak and cold,
And still the dead leaves flutter down
As the years grow old.
And still — forever gravely fair —
Beneath their fitful whirl,
New England's sweetest girl,
Rose Standish, takes the air.

III.

HARVEST.

SWEET, sweet, sweet,
 Is the wind's song,
Astir in the rippled wheat
 All day long.
It hath the brook's wild gayety,
The sorrowful cry of the sea.
 Oh hush and hear !
 Sweet, sweet and clear,
 Above the locust's whirr
 And hum of bee
Rises that soft, pathetic harmony.

In the meadow-grass
  The innocent white daisies blow,
The dandelion plume doth pass
  Vaguely to and fro —
The unquiet spirit of a flower
That hath too brief an hour.

Now doth a little cloud all white,
  Or golden bright,
Drift down the warm, blue sky;
  And now on the horizon line
Where dusky woodlands lie,
  A sunny mist doth shine,
Like to a veil before a holy shrine,
  Concealing, half-revealing
    Things Divine.

Sweet, sweet, sweet,
  Is the wind's song,
Astir in the rippled wheat
  All day long.

That exquisite music calls
 The reaper everywhere —
 Life and death must share,
The golden harvest falls.

So doth all end —
 Honored Philosophy,
 Science and Art,
 The bloom of the heart ; —
Master, Consoler, Friend,
 Make Thou the harvest of our days
 To fall within thy ways.

IV.

THE RUNAWAY.

Joy, my tender fairy,
Wilful, wistful, airy —
I pray you, tell me why
You are so very shy.

Don't I want you, love you,
Look and long to prove you
Friend, as I to you,
Faithful, gentle, true?

" You don't know how to find me;
You don't know how to bind me;

I fly, yet am not shy —
Shall I tell you why?

" Because, while you pursue,
My sweetness I renew;
I fold my wings to rest
In some less eager breast!"

V.

SO WAGS THE WORLD.

MEMORY cannot linger long,
  Joy must die the death.
Hope 's like a little silver song
  Fading in a breath.
So wags the weary world away
  Forever and a day.

But love, that sweetest madness,
Leaps and grows in toil and sadness,
Makes unseeing eyes to see,
And heapeth wealth in penury.
So wags the good old world away
  Forever and a day.

VI.

AT THE PALACE-GATE.

IF at thy palace-gate,
Dear, thou dost bid me wait
And take such dole of love
As thy calm heart may move,
In truth, I have no way
Nor will to say thee nay.

If from my living heart,
Love, thou dost bid me part,
And leaving it with thee
Keep only memory, —
Alas ! I have no way
Nor will to say thee nay.

VII.

SEA-WAY.

THE tide slips up the silver sand,
　　Dark night and rosy day;
It brings sea-treasures to the land,
　　Then bears them all away.
On mighty shores from east to west
It wails, and gropes, and cannot rest.

O Tide, that still doth ebb and flow
　　Through night to golden day: —
Wit, learning, beauty, come and go,
　　Thou giv'st — thou tak'st away.
But sometime, on some gracious shore,
Thou shalt lie still and ebb no more.

———

VIII.

AT SEA.

FLYING down into the dark,
Cloudy schooner, brig, and bark,
Flit away beyond the bar,
Melting, fading, far and far —
  Flying down into the dark.

Flying fast from strand to strand,
Spurning ocean, spurning land,
A sea-bird wheels in ardent quest.
Pr'ythee, brother, canst not rest ? —
  Flying fast from strand to strand.

Flying far beyond the blue,

Thought's a wilful wanderer too;

Love, dost draw my dreams thy way?

All in vain I bid them stay —

Flying far beyond the blue.

IX.

A FLOWER'S EPITAPH.

THESE dead leaves were a violet once,
  A tender, timid thing,
A sleeping beauty till the wind
  Kissed it awake in Spring.

Then for one little, little hour
  It knew Love's deep delight;
Unto the wooing wind it gave
  All that a violet might.

And then it drooped and faded happily;
For having loved, it was not pain to die.

X.

PRISCILLA.

My little Love sits in the shade
  Beneath the climbing roses,
And gravely sews in a half-dream
The dainty measures of her seam
  Until the twilight closes.

I look and long, yet have no care
  To break her maiden musing;
I idly toss my book away,
And watch her pretty fingers stray
  Along their task confusing.

The dews fall, and the sunset light
  Goes creeping o'er the meadows,
And still, with serious eyes cast down,
She gravely sews her wedding-gown
  Among the growing shadows.

I needs must gaze, though on her cheek
  The bashful roses quiver —
She is so modest, simple, sweet,
That I, poor pilgrim, at her feet
  Would fain adore forever.

A heavenly peace dwells in her heart;
  Her love is yet half duty.
Serene and serious, still and quaint,
She 's partly woman, partly saint,
  This Presbyterian beauty.

She is so shy that all my prayers
  Scarce win a few small kisses —

She lifts her lovely eyes to mine
And softly grants, with blush divine,
  Such slender grace as this is.

I watch her with a tender care
  And joy not free from sadness —
For what am I that I should take
This gentle soul and think to make
  Its future days all gladness?

Can I fulfil those maiden dreams
  In some imperfect fashion?
I am no hero, but I know
I love you, Dear — the rest I throw
  Upon your sweet compassion.

———

XI.

THE SWEET BETRAYAL.

My darling tries with all her art
To hide young Love within her heart,
But, prisoned in that tender nest,
He frets, and frets, and will not rest;
And soon the little rogue I spy
At play within her laughing eye.

My darling tries with all her skill
To bind young Love unto her will,
But work such witchcraft as she may,
The pretty rebel hath his way.
He decks her cheeks with blushes rare,
And lingers in the dimples there ; —
In glance and blush and smile I spy
All that my love would fain deny.

XII.

THE DATE IN THE RING.

THE women dressed her for farewell
  In snowy silk and lace ;
A crown of her braided hair they set
  Above her quiet face,
And on her placid breast they laid
White roses, as became a maid.

Her mother bent and kissed her lips,
  And kissed her braided hair,
And folded down the peaceful hands
  Upon the bosom fair,
And, weeping, saw on one a ring—
A little golden, time-worn thing.

She took it from the icy hand
  And looked for rhyme or name —
Something to say why it was there,
  From whose fond thought it came.
She only saw, through many a tear,
A date long past — day, month, and year.

" 'T was some schoolfellow's gift," she sighed,
  " The child forgot to show,"
And put it back in its own place
  With tender touch and slow,
And saw its tiny glitter rest
  Like sunshine on that quiet breast.

Ah, little ring, you kept it well,
  The secret of your date !
Whatever its meaning, it goes untold
  Beyond the earth and fate :
Pain or blessing — who can say
How much of either in it lay ?

We watch the light in our darlings' eyes,
　The lines that the slow years bring,
Yet know as little what they mean
　As the secret of the ring.
Joy or sorrow — God only knows
How much of both lies under the rose.

———

XIII.

IN SNOW.

THE golden meadows sleep in snow;
The arrowy winds about them blow,
And icy sparkles come and go.

The golden meadows sleep in snow;
But underneath the grasses grow,
And daisies dream of bud and blow.

The golden meadows sleep in snow;
My little maiden, dost thou know
How half unconscious love may grow?

XIV.

SHADOW SONG.

THE silver dew hath come again
  To garden, hill, and meadow:
It is the shadow of the rain —
  A shimmering soft shadow.

The cool white moonlight hath its will
  With wood and glistening meadow:
'T is sunshine's shadow, pale and still,
  A mystical, sweet shadow.

My Queen the shining path doth take
  Across the misty meadow;
I follow for her darling sake —
  For I am but her shadow.

———

XV.

ON THE ROAD.

DOST know the way to Paradise ?
  Pray, tell me, by thy grace.
" Any way thou canst devise
  That leads to my Love's face —
  For that 's his dwelling-place."

How far is it to Paradise ?
  " Ah, that I cannot say ;
Time loiters and my heart it flies —
  A minute seems a day
  Whene'er I go that way."

XVI.

NOCTURNE.

WAN Twilight in her gown of gray
Comes swiftly down the western way,
    With Moonshine hastening after ;
And here among the forest damps
She lights her twinkling firefly lamps,
    And stills the wind's wild laughter.

The brook in trilling monotone
Gives sleepy welcome of its own,
    The cedars bend and quiver,
But all the meadow sounds are still,
The flocks are folded on the hill
    Beyond the placid river.

Sweet Twilight, as thou com'st to these
With healing dew and soothing breeze,
  So come thou unto me.
Bring gentle dreams and quiet rest,
Weave, weave thy spell, O shadowy guest,
  In calm benignity !

XVII.

WIND-FLOWER.

I THOUGHT to find my darling waiting in the
    wood —
Did anybody see her, to-day or yesterday?
    She wears a snowy gown,
    And the softest cloak of down.
It 's a timid air she has, and a modest little way.

It 's no use to ask the Wind, for he 's jealous of
    my dear ;
He wants her for himself, and he wooes her all
    the time ;

But woo her all he dare,

My darling does n't care, —

She shakes her little head to his reason and his
rhyme.

I thought to find her hidden in the brown and
rustling leaves;

The days are long and sunny warm, where can
my treasure stay?

— Ah, here you are, my sweet,

Here, smiling at my feet,

Spite of all your timid air, and your modest little
way!

XVIII.

O GOLDEN ARROW.

O GOLDEN arrow on the spire,
Yield'st thou to the Wind's desire?
— To the southward veering, turning,
In the crimson sunset burning.

O heart, why stir in sad desire —
Burn'st thou within Love's altar-fire?
— To the southward vainly turning,
For thine own Beloved yearning!

———

XIX.

THE SENTINEL.

HE paces round the fortress wall
   For hours and hours together ;
Afar his ringing footsteps fall ;
   Through wild and wintry weather
He paces round the fortress wall
   Hours and hours together.

So Love doth guard the loving heart
   For years and years together.
Grief cannot stay, nor anger start,
   Whatever be life's weather.
So Love doth guard the loving heart
   Years and years together.

———

XX.

BLUE FLAGS.

FLEUR DE LIS.

WHAT sweet rebellion in thy blood,
  My June, hath bid thee raise
Thy royal standards by the wood
  And through the meadow ways?
What stir of passion, darling sprite,
Spread these blue banners to the light?

Past lily buds and leafy blades
  The glorious pageant flies:
In sunny shallows, reedy shades,
  Unnumbered blossoms rise.

By rocky coast, in salty bight,
Thy banners glitter in the light.

Wrought of warm noons and morning dew,
  And painted from the skies,
Say, have they not the very blue
  Of Maiden Marian's eyes?
Ah, June, thy flags are not so bright
As those deep eyes are in the light!

XXI.

A DAY IN SPRING.

LITTLE violets in the garden staying,
  Small and blue, and sweet as sweet can be,
Don't you wonder what it is we 're playing
  Up in the world? Suppose you come and see.

We play at joy, and find our play no pleasure;
  We play at faith, and quickly throw it by;
We play at hope, and think our toy a treasure
  Until Time shows it scarcely worth a sigh.

Little violets in the garden staying,
  Small and blue, and sweet as sweet can be,
Do you wonder what it is we 're playing?
  Wake up, darlings! Pray you, come and see.

XXII.

THE SHADOW.

IF he once were dear,
Oh, if he once were dear —
Love cannot die and be forgotten quite.
If he hath grieving lain
At the feet of Pain,
The tired heart still keeps his memory bright.

A gentle ghost, he sits
At frozen hearths, and flits,
Quiet and calm, beside the desolate way;
And still the sweet appeal
His shadowy eyes reveal
Takes heart and soul back to a happier day.

.

XXIII.

MARCH SONGS.

I.

ALOFT, alow, the mad winds blow ;
On fields and uplands bare
They seize the lingering wreaths of snow,
And hurl and whirl them to and fro,
And heap them here and there.

Round the deserted garden-ways
Where last year's lilies lie,
The savage North-wind, shrieking, strays,
And there the wilful West-wind plays
With flower-stalks dun and dry.

Blow, blow, wild winds, aloft, alow !
   The ides of March are past ;
Swift as your wings the dark days go,
Then blow your maddest, winds, blow, blow !
   My May is coming fast.

II.

WAX and wane, once and again,
   O pallid moon of March !
Swifter lift thy light and drift
   Across the sky's blue arch.

Wax and wane, once and again,
   Till April 's fled away ;
Speed, speed thy flight through night to night,
   And be the moon of May.

XXIV.

FOR LOVE IS BLIND.

FATE counselled her if she were wise
To set a guard upon her eyes,
And thus be safe from Love's surprise.

But Youth, the hero, came erelong,
Came singing through a heedless throng; —
She listened, breathless, to his song.

"O Fate," she murmured, "wert thou wise?
I set a guard upon mine eyes,
Yet must I yield to Love's surprise!"

XXV.

A LOVER'S ANSWER.

An early rose, a late rose —
　　What matters it, mine own,
　　Since all its gracious beauty
　　Blooms for you alone?
An early rose is of the dawn, dewy, fleeting,
　　　　bright;
A late rose is of the noon, a lingering delight.

First love, last love —
　　What does it matter, dear,
　　Since for your maiden grace it pleads
　　In earnest faith and fear?
First love is of the dawn, dewy, fleeting, bright;
Last love is of the noon, life's lingering delight.

XXVI.

THE DIFFERENCE.

THE budding boughs before him bent
   In the dark and the rain,
As carelessly he turned and went
   Down the lonely lane.
And drifting with the wind's wild cry
She heard: "Good-by, fair friend, good-by."

At the door she idly stayed
   And watched the twilight wane
Through the arch the wet boughs made
   Above the dreary lane.
Ah, sodden earth and darkening sky!
She wept, "Good-by, my Love, good-by."

Through the rain and the wind he went
  Into the world again.
Fate and Fortune before him bent,
  Forgot was the lonely lane.
Only the night-wind heard her cry —
  " Alas ! Good-by, my Love, good-by."

XXVII.

APRIL FANTASIE.

THE fresh, bright bloom of the daffodils
Makes gold in the garden bed,
Gold that is like the sunbeams
Loitering overhead.
Bloom, bloom
In the sun and the wind —
April hath a fickle mind.

The budding twigs of the sweetbrier
Stir as with hope and bliss
Under the sun's soft glances,
Under the wind's sly kiss.
Swing, swing
In the sun and the wind —
April hath a fickle mind.

May, she calls to her little ones,
Her flowers hiding away,
" Never put off till to-morrow
What you may do to-day.
Come, come
Through the sun and the wind —
April hath a fickle mind."

XXVIII.

THE PRINCE.

SEPTEMBER waves his golden-rod
　　Along the lanes and hollows,
And saunters round the sunny fields
　　A-playing with the swallows.

The corn has listened for his step,
　　The maples blush to greet him,
And gay, coquetting Sumach dons
　　Her velvet cloak to meet him.

Come to the hearth, O merry Prince,
　　With flaming knot and ember;
For all your tricks of frosty eves,
　　We love your ways, September!

———

XXIX.

ALL THE YEAR ROUND.

Go, time and tide, go as you will —
  I cannot heed your ways.
What care I for summer glow,
What care I for ice and snow,
  When love doth fill my days?

Unto its ark through wind and rain
  My heart flies as the dove;
Oh, rosy is the darkened day
And rosy is the stormy way
  That lead me to my Love.

How can I care if leaves be green
  Or gray with early rime?
Love, ruling, reigning in the soul
With pure and passionate control,
  Makes its own summer-time!

———

XXX.

LOVE'S IMAGINATION.

" A little Western flower — "

THERE is a pretty herb that grows
  In the everywhere.
The chilliest wild winter snows,
  The roughest saucy air,
  It hath a way to dare,
And kissed by warmest wind that blows
  It blooms as fairy fair.
Yet though it grow on every side,
No mortal knows where it doth bide.
One seeks in vain till locks be gray;
And one, upon some happy day,
Unheeding, finds it in his way.

Hast found the wildling, my Lucile?
 Ah, do not pluck it, Sweet;
If but one dainty touch it feel,
 It withers at thy feet!

XXXI.

THE QUEST.

IT was a heavenly time of life
  When first I went to Spain,
The lovely land of silver mists,
  The land of golden grain.

My little ship through unknown seas
  Sailed many a changing day;
Sometimes the chilling winds came up
  And blew across her way.

Sometimes the rain came down and hid
  The shining shores of Spain,
The beauty of the silver mists '
  And of the golden grain.

But through the rains and through the winds,
  Upon the untried sea,
My fairy ship sailed on and on,
  With all my dreams and me.

And now, no more a child, I long
  For that sweet time again,
When on the far horizon bar
  Rose up the shores of Spain.

O lovely land of silver mists,
  O land of golden grain,
I look for you with smiles, with tears,
  But look for you in vain!

———

XXXII.

MAY MORNING SONGS.

I.

WHEN Chanticleer in early morn
Winds his keen and merry horn,
Meadow-mists, all pale and shy,
After moonshine, fading, fly;
Dew-wet daffodils arise,
Pansies open their dark eyes;
Apple-blossoms far and near
Unlock their dainty buds to hear.
Dream and midnight phantasy
To haunt of elf and goblin hie,
Or make a forty-minute dart
To vex some drowsy Chinese heart.
Floods of shimmering sunshine play
Around the world and make it May!

II.

Rosy clouds fled round the sky,
The little joyous Winds rushed by,
In greening woods to wake the Day,
And it was May!

Her blue eyes opened sweet and slow,—
The violet buds began to blow;
She smiled, and in a sudden flame
The tulips came!

———

XXXIII.

TRYST.

" There is a willow grows ascaunt the brook,
  That shows his hoar leaves in the glassy stream — "

UNDER the willow on a summer day,
  He watched the breaking bubbles on the
    stream,
Eager, impatient, chiding eve's delay,
For one soft footstep list'ning till the gray,
  Cool twilight, falling, held him like a dream.

The gentle stars came out, but she, of all
  The fairest star, shone not upon his dark;
He felt the tender dew begin to fall;
He heard a nestling's faint and sleepy call,
  And saw the firefly light his radiant spark.

—O cruel Fate! the thread is cut you spun.

He sees a fair face in the shadows gleam :—

Pale, pale, poor girl — her little day is done ;

Kissed by the careless ripples as they run,

She comes to meet him, tossing in the stream.

———

XXXIV.

MARGUERITE.

FROM dawn to nightfall at her window sitting,
  She waits, while drift the heavy hours away;
And like the swallows all her thoughts go flitting
  To that sweet South wherein they fain would
    stay.

Up from the street there comes the lazy laughter
  Of girls who linger by the fountain's fall;
She heeds them not — her gaze still follows after
  The clouds that roll beyond the city wall.

She vaguely hears her mother's fretful chiding,
  Her idle wheel grows dusty at her side;
Listless she wonders where her love is biding:
  Where'er he be there must her heart abide.

All the day long she listens for his coming,
  All the long day she dreams of one dear face;
She hears his whisper in the bees' low humming,
  She feels his kisses in the wind's embrace.

Lonely she dreams while the warm sunshine lingers
  Upon the carven angels of her chair —
Alone sits sobbing, while with silver fingers
  The moonbeams thread her soft unbraided hair·

Ah, heavy heart! so passionate its yearning,
  She needs must know that all her peace is o'er ;
That eager pain 'neath her white bosom burning
  Tells her 't is gone, to enter there no more;

But once to feel, unchecked, his fond caressing!
  One wild, sweet hour close to his heart to press!
There her thought stops; what else of bliss or
    blessing
  The great world holds she does not care to
    guess.

Still at her window, dreaming, longing, weeping,
  While to their mates the gray doves coo and
    call,
She leans and watches the slow clouds go
    creeping
  Far down the blue, beyond the city wall.

———

XXXV.

AUTUMN SONG.

RED leaf, gold leaf,
Flutter down the wind:
Life is brief, oh! life is brief,
But Mother Earth is kind;
From her dear bosom ye shall spring
To new blossoming.

The red leaf, the gold leaf,
They have had their way;
Love is long if life be brief, —
Life is but a day;
And Love from Grief and Death shall spring
To new blossoming.

———

XXXVI.

SUMMER NIGHT.

LEND me thy lance, O gracious moon,
  That I may cleave the dark;
Sing softer, wind, or hush thy tune;
  O laughing river, hark!

For I have lost my heart, alas!
  And know that it is near.
— O tangled vine-leaves, let him pass, —
  He comes, my dear! my dear!

XXXVII.

QUAKER LADIES.

[In New England the Houstonia is known as the
"Quaker Lady."]

MORE shy than the shy violet,
   Hiding when the wind doth pass,
   Nestled in the nodding grass,
With morning mist all wet,
   In open woodland ways
   The Quaker Lady strays.

Pale as noonday cloudlets are,
   Floating in the blue,
This little wildwood star
   Blooms in light and dew.

Sun and shadow on her hair,
   Flowers about her feet,
   Pale and still and sweet;
As a nun all pure and fair,
Through the soft spring air,
   In the light of God
   Deborah walks abroad.

Her little cap it hath a grace
   Most demure and grave,
And her kerchief's modest lace
   Veils the lovely wave
Above her maiden heart,
Where only gentle thoughts have part.
   Even the tying of her shoe
   Hath beauty in it too,
A delicate, sweet art.

Hiding when the wind goes by,
   Not afraid, yet shy,

The tiny flower takes from the sky
Life's own light and dew,
And its exquisite hue.
And the little Quaker maid
Timidly, yet not afraid,
Unfolds the sweetness of her soul
To Heavenly control,
And wears upon her quiet face
The Spirit's tender grace.

XXXVIII.

THE WAYS OF LOVE.

SWEET and bitter together, —
  That is our portion here;
Love that is truth, growth, spirit, —
  That is the sweet, my dear.

Sweet and bitter together, —
  Reproach and scorn and fear;
Love that forgives not, endures not, —
  That is the bitter, my dear.

Sweet and bitter together, —
  That is our portion here.
Thank Him who on one side the river
  Gives us only the sweet, my dear.

XXXIX.

OLIVIA.

WITH flout and pout and pretty frown
  For this, for that, Olivia teased;
I kissed her cheek, and smiled her down
  Until her saucy urging ceased
And angry tears shone in her eyes,
With: "Nay, my love, it were not wise,
  My fair Olivia."

But soon, with this and that forgot,
  I wooed my bright Olivia's smiles:
She turned to sunshine on the spot;
  I fell before her fairy wiles!
— Yet wondered then, and wonder still
How 't was she got her own sweet will,
  My wife, Olivia.

————

XL.

LILAC.

I CANNOT tell why lilac flowers
    Should bring me such strange dreams:
Within their scented purple buds
    A wondrous witchcraft gleams.

It pictures languid Persian girls,
    Star-Eyes and Rose-in-Bloom,
The jewel-clusters gathering
    In Orient garden-gloom.

Then in a still New England lane,
    Beneath the starlight wan,
My errant fancy stays to kiss
    A dove-eyed Puritan.

Ah, Lilac, in your pretty art
　You give me of the best, —
The passion of the Orient,
　The sweetness of the West !

XLI.

A SUMMER RAIN.

THE rippling music of the shower is still ;
  Low, thunderous murmurs tremble in the west ;
A listless breeze now stirs the dripping leaves,
  Now wafts a perfume from its crimson nest.
Bright blooms the rose, bright waves the ripen-
      ing grain,
Crowned with the blessing of the summer rain.

The solemn elm-tree shakes its ancient locks
  In grave monotony above the stream ;
From all its branches roll the shining drops,
  Dimpling the water with a transient gleam.
Upon the earth the hand of God hath lain, —
His benediction is the summer rain.

So in my heart the summer lives and glows,
　And in its light soft shine the coming years;
I lie and dream through many a golden day—
　Ah happy dreams that bring such happy tears!
No joy was e'er so sweet as this sweet pain—
Gleaming through sunshine falls the summer rain.

———

XLII.

ALL IN ALL.

HER Love, he hath a lordly way,
  He knoweth how to chide ;
But 't is no grievance to obey, —
  She sees in him her guide.

His frown doth hurt her to the heart,
  Yet she would not rebel ;
She could not see 't, were they apart,
  So she doth love it well.

The music of his voice can lose
  Naught in its sternest change ;
Then, though he chide, she cannot choose
  Her loving to estrange.

XLIII.

NOVEMBER DAYS.

FLYING, flying —
I watch the swallows flying,
  Flitting south before November snows,
Leaving the delaying leaves a-dying
  Broken-hearted for the buried rose.

Follow, follow —
Everything must follow ; —
  Even the memory of the summer dies.
Follow, follow ; good-by, happy swallow,
  Flying southward as the summer flies.

XLIV.

TO-MORROW.

O SUMMER day, that art so brief,
From Earth her utmost beauty borrow,
With wildwood song and fragrant leaf
Weave happy visions of To-morrow!
O fair To-day,
That will not stay,
Leave some bright vision of To-morrow!

O winter day, that art so long,
Canst not from flying summer borrow
Some fancied bloom and light and song,
Some heavenly vision of To-morrow!
O desolate day
That must away,
Leave some bright vision of To-morrow!

XLV.

LOVE IN HERMITAGE.

BEHIND closed doors and double locks he bides,
  The little anchorite, grave, serene, and sweet,
With radiant wings hid 'neath monastic guise,
  And quiver laid, forgotten, at his feet.
A wreath of thorns, a knotted scourge, hath he,
And drops of flame that are his rosary.

Year after year the mayflowers smile and die;
  O'er wild-rose hedges summer breezes blow;
The last frail gentian nods forlorn adieus,
  And winter snows drift ghostly to and fro.
"Hath summer come?"   "Is winter here?"
        saith he,
  And, musing, turns him to his rosary.

Each ruby bead gleams with a secret fire,
  Each the brief history of a tilt with life;
This, tragic passion — this, a dear despair —
  This, dream of rest that is to end the strife.
" What griefs, what joys, lie prisoned here," saith
    he,
  And tells his prayers upon his rosary.

The soul it is that guards this hermitage;
  The busy world, unseeing, passes by,
Counts up its losses, balances its gains,
  Unconscious of a treasure hidden nigh.
Sweet Love laughs softly.   " Life is short," saith
    he,
" And to the grave I give my rosary."

XLVI.

A CRY FROM THE SHORE.

COME down, ye graybeard mariners,
   Unto the wasting shore !
The morning winds are up, — the gods
   Bid me to dream no more.
Come, tell me whither I must sail,
   What peril there may be,
Before I take my life in hand
   And venture out to sea !

" We may not tell thee where to sail,
   Nor what the dangers are ;
Each sailor soundeth for himself,
   Each hath a separate star :
Each sailor soundeth for himself,
   And on the awful sea

What we have learned is ours alone;
  We may not tell it thee."

Come back, O ghostly mariners,
  Ye who have gone before!
I dread the dark, impetuous tides;
  I dread the farther shore.
Tell me the secret of the waves;
  Say what my fate shall be —
Quick! for the mighty winds are up,
  And will not wait for me.

"Hail and farewell, O voyager!
  Thyself must read the waves;
What we have learned of sun and storm
  Lies with us in our graves:
What we have learned of sun and storm
  Is ours alone to know.
The winds are blowing out to sea,
  Take up thy life and go!"

XLVII.

MORNING-GLORY.

FLOWER-O'-FLAX is like the sky,
Or an innocent maiden's eye ;
Lilies, too, are very fair,
And larkspur hath a regal air ;
The red rose wooes the wind afar ;
Marigold 's a fairy star ;
All debonair and full of cheer,
Sweet-William 's a gay cavalier ;
Yet dearer than these you are, my pretty sweeting,
My Morning-glory, dainty-fine and fleeting !

Where last year's withered branches bide,
There doth my Beauty twine and hide :
That clinging tendril's soft caress
Might move a stone to tenderness.

At dawn her lovely lids unclose

To shame the clouds with pearl and rose.

All a flower knows of fresh and sweet

In these bewitching blossoms meet.

Oh, dearest of all you are, my pretty sweeting,

My Morning-glory, dainty-fine and fleeting !

XLVIII.

THE HIDDEN CHARM.

WHETHER my life be glad or no,
The summers come, the summers go.
The lanes grow dark with dying leaves;
Icicles hang beneath the eaves;
The asters wither to the snow:
    Thus doth the summer end and go,
    Whether my life be glad or no.

Whether my life be sad or no,
The winters come, the winters go.
The sunshine plays with baby leaves;
Swallows build about the eaves;
Violets in the woodland blow:
    Thus doth the winter end and go,
    Whether my life be sad or no.

Yet Mother Nature gives to me
A fond and patient sympathy;
In my own heart I find the charm
To make her tender, near, and warm;
Through summer sunshine, winter snow,
She clasps me, sad or glad or no.

XLIX.

UNDER THE STARS.

O NIGHT, look down through cloud and star
    Upon our fret and pain!
Bid all the dreams that day denies
    Bloom into faith again!
In silvery shades of shadow come
And take Earth's weary children home!

Sweet teacher, wiser than the schools,
    Thy speechless lessons bring;
The rebel soul, the aching heart,
    The will like broken wing,
Make ready for a stiller night,
And for a dearer Morning Light!

L.

VAGRANT PANSIES.

THEY are all in the lily bed, cuddled close to-
    gether —
Purples, Yellow Cap, and little Baby Blue ;
How they ever got there you must ask the April
    weather,
  The morning and the evening winds, the sun-
    shine and the dew.

Why they should go visiting the tall and haughty
    lilies
  Is very odd, and none of them will condescend
    to say ;

They might have made a call upon the jolly daf-
    fodillies —
They might have come to my house any pleas-
    ant day.

They don't have a good time, I think, their little
    faces
Look so very solemn underneath each velvet
    hood;
I wonder don't they feel among the garden's airs
    and graces
That shy Cousin Violet is happier in the wood?

Ah, my pretty Pansies, it 's no use to go a-seek-
    ing;
There is n't any good time waiting anywhere;
I fancy even Violet is troubled — mildly speak-
    ing —
When somebody plucks her, finding her so
    fair.

There 's nothing left for you, my pets, but just to
    do your duty:
  Bloom, and make the world bright, — that 's
    the best for you;
There is n't much that 's lovelier than your bash-
    ful beauty,
  My Purples, my Yellow Cap, my little Baby
    Blue.

LI.

JUNE.

OF silvery-shining rains
  And noonday golds and shadows
June weaves wild-daisy chains
  For the happy meadows.

She stoops to set the stream
  With scented alder-bushes,
And with the rainbow gleam
  Of iris 'mid the rushes.
She scatters eglantine
And scarlet columbine.

Ah, June, my lovely lass, —
  Sweetheart, dost thou not see
I stay to watch thee pass —
  What hast thou brought to me?

Thy mystic ministries
Of glorious far skies,
Thy wild-rose sermons, Sweet,
Like dreams profound and fleet,
  Thy woodland harmony
  Thou givest me.

The vision that can see,
  The loving will to learn,
How fair thy skies may be,
  What in thy roses burn,
Thy secret harmonies, —
Ah, give me these !

LII.

MIDSUMMER SONG.

Now flits the bee through clover-dales,
  Now shallow grows the river
In leafy nooks where lilies float
  And wandering sunbeams quiver.
Now thistledown begins to fly,
And drowsily the South winds sigh,
    "Good-by, good-by,
      Good-by."

O fair Midsummer! Like the bee
  Adream in sylvan places,
We taste the sweetness of thy bloom,
  Thy wonderful, wild graces.
Alas! must all this beauty die?
— Drowsily the soft winds sigh,
    "Good-by, good-by,
      Good-by."